T0131996

Donuts Don't Lie

By ANGELA WILKINSON   Illustrations by Gil Balbuena Jr.

Print information available on the last page

Rev. date: 05/22/2015

To order additional copies of this book, contact:
Xlibris
1-888-795-4274
www.Xlibris.com
Orders@Xlibris.com

Donuts Don't Lie

By ANGELA WILKINSON

Mom was in the kitchen, making a grocery list, while Dad and Tay-Tay were in the family room. Dad was watching sports on TV, and Tay-Tay was playing with his toys, secretly daydreaming of powdered donuts. He tasted them for the first time at his day care yesterday afternoon. He just can't stop thinking about those powdered donuts that melt in his mouth.

"Honey, I'm going to the grocery store," Mom called out to Dad.

"Okay, dear. Drive carefully," Dad replied.

Tay-Tay heard the words *grocery store* and got excited. He ran into the kitchen and stood next to Mom with a huge smile on his face. "Oooh! Can I go with you?" he asked as he tugged on Mom's dress.

Mom grinned. "Sure, honey. I'll wait for you while you put on your shoes."

He ran back into the family room to put his shoes on quick, fast, and in a hurry. All the while, he was dreaming of those powdered donuts. Tay-Tay had a plan.

Mom buckled Tay-Tay safely in his booster seat and gave it a tug to make sure it was secure. She did the same after she buckled her seat belt. Off to the grocery store they went.

When they arrived at Beckam's Grocery Store, Tay-Tay could barely contain himself. "Whew! That was a long ride."

"Seven minutes is not long at all. You must be excited about something inside this grocery store," Mom said as she unbuckled her seat belt. Tay-Tay bared a smile that covered everything except his eyes. They both laughed as Mom unbuckled his booster seat.

Once inside, Tay-Tay ran straight for the grocery cart that looked like a racecar. He got in the driver's side and closed the door. He stuck his hand out of the window and gave his mom a thumbs-up and said, "Let's go!" Mom chuckled as she pushed the cart toward the fruits and vegetables. After going down three boring aisles, Mom finally went down the aisle with the sweet treats. Halfway down the aisle, Tay-Tay spotted the powdered donuts. "Beep, beep! Beep, beep!" he shouted. "Stop, Mom! I see them!"

"You see what, Tay-Tay?"

"The donuts! The powdered ones. Can I get them? Can I, can I? Pretty please?" he begged.

"I don't see why you can't get them. Here, I'll let you hold them until we pay for them." Mom always let Tay-Tay get one special treat of his choice when they go grocery shopping together.

"Thanks, Mom!"

"You're very welcome, dear."

On the ride home, Tay-Tay was still holding the powdered donuts. He couldn't wait to eat one. When they got home, he asked his mom if he could have one. She politely told him that he would have to wait until after dinner. Tay-Tay was disappointed. He didn't think he could wait until after dinner. He had waited so long already. Mom put away the groceries and prepared dinner. She placed the covered dish in the oven and joined Dad on the sofa until dinner was ready.

Tay-Tay had to do something to get his mind off those donuts. He decided to play football by himself until it was time for dinner. He grabbed the football from his toy chest and started running all throughout the house. Although he was having fun, he was still thinking about those powdered donuts. The thought of them being in the house drove him silly! He couldn't take it anymore. He just couldn't wait another minute. He snuck in the pantry, opened the donuts, and put one in his mouth. *"Ahhhhhh, these are soooooooo good!"* he thought to himself. He felt relieved that he had finally tasted one of the donuts. He started to run around again. He happily made his way into the living room and stood in front of his parents and yelled, "Touchdown!" His parents clapped their hands and cheered for him.

As he was about to run back out of the room, Dad stopped him by tugging on the back of his shirt. "Whoa. Hold on, little fella. Have you been eating those powdered donuts?"

"Huh?" asked Tay-Tay.

"You heard me. Have you been eating those powdered donuts?" Dad repeated.

With a serious face and fast heartbeat, Tay-Tay replied with a shaky voice, "N-no."

"You know, son, donuts don't lie!"

Looking confused with his nose crinkled up, Tay-Tay responded again, "Huh?"

"Go look in the bathroom mirror," Dad instructed.

Tay-Tay dashed straight for the bathroom. He stood on the step stool and looked in the mirror. Dad was right. Donuts don't lie. He saw the white powder from the donuts all over his face. All he could do was throw his head back and start crying.

"Whaaaaaaaaaaaaa!"

Mom and Dad sat on the sofa as they listened to Tay-Tay wail. Finally, Dad said, "Son, come here. Mom and I need to talk to you."

Tay-Tay walked slowly into the family room with his head hanging low. He felt very sad. He had never lied to his parents before. He was afraid to look them in their eyes. Dad gently lifted Tay-Tay's chin with his fingers then motioned for him to sit down on the sofa. Dad talked to Tay-Tay about the importance of always telling the truth and how harmful it is to tell lies. He explained that even when people who tell lies finally tell the truth, it's hard for others to believe them.

Afterward, Tay-Tay hugged his parents and apologized for not telling the truth. He promised not to ever lie again.

His parents accepted Tay-Tay's apology. However, there was a lesson to be learned. Mom said, "Because you didn't tell the truth, you will not have any more donuts after dinner. You'll have to wait until after dinner tomorrow. In addition, you will not be able to get a special treat the next time we go to the grocery store. Is that clear?"

"Yes, ma'am," said Tay-Tay.

Later that night, after his bath, Tay-Tay crawled into bed and thought about the lesson he learned. He still felt sad for not telling the truth. However, the thought of eating those powdered donuts after dinner tomorrow made him feel much better. Tay-Tay placed both hands behind his head, closed his eyes, and counted powdered donuts until he fell asleep.

Printed in the United States
By Bookmasters